A. F. Scott, a mother of five children, was diagnosed with vascular brain lesions, multiple sclerosis and fibromyalgia. Her whole life changed; she became more aware of the lack of understanding about dementia and decided she would like to write a children's book to raise awareness. She also turned to poetry to express her feelings. One of her poems called 'Leaving You' was published in a book called *Silent Voices*. Scott lives with her ten-year-old daughter, Evie, who is Scott's carer. She is currently working on more *Evie's Mummy* and *Sizzling Bacon Adventures*.

SIZZLING BACON

A. F. SCOTT

AUST'N MACAULEY PUBLISHERS™
LONDON • CAMBRIDGE • NEW YORK • SHARJAH

A CIP catalogue record for this title is available from the British Library.

ISBN 9781528994552 (Paperback)
ISBN 9781528994569 (ePub e-book)

www.austinmacauley.com

First Published (2020)
Austin Macauley Publishers Ltd
25 Canada Square
Canary Wharf
London
E14 5LQ

To those travelling the dementia path – may you find happiness in the darkness.

To my children, Jason, Mark, Christopher, Tiana and Evie, who are all awesome. A big thank you for the help, encouragement and support you showed, which was monumental in the completion of this book. I love you all!

Evie woke up from her lovely sleep and wondered to herself why she could not smell the delicious aroma of lovely, hot, sizzling bacon wafting up the stairs to her, and more importantly why were her bedclothes so heavy?

Evie could not understand why her cosy bed had suddenly become so uncomfortable. Evie tried to move her little legs but she had to struggle really hard to move them even a tiny bit and when she did, she heard loud clunking noises.

Evie was terrified! She just could not understand why her cosy, blue, fluffy blanket could suddenly be so heavy; she felt frightened and wondered if some sort of huge, ugly monster had eaten all of her lovely sizzling bacon to make him so heavy, then creeped in and was now sitting on her bed watching her maybe waiting to eat her too.

Evie was so glad that she had her lovely fluffy blanket pulled right up to her little button nose and the monster would not be able to see her.

As Evie had these thoughts, she lay very still. Her heart was beating so fast she could hear it in her ears, Evie was too scared to move or to look just in case the monster was real, and snarled with his huge teeth at her, but Evie knew she had to get out of bed as it was Christmas eve and she didn't want to waste a second of the day.

Evie decided she would need to be very brave so she clutched the blue, fluffy duvet even tighter around herself and shouted in a very loud voice, "There is no such thing as 'monsters'. Monsters do not exist … I do not believe in monsters. I am going to close my eyes tightly and when I open them you will be gone." As she did this, Evie bravely opened one eye and peeped over the top of her duvet.

Looking down the bed she discovered all of last night's dinner dishes, all of the pots and pans, all of the knives and forks, all of the plates and cups were all sitting on her bed. Evie let out a loud relieved laugh. Her little heart was still pounding from fear of the monster being real but she knew that was silly; there wasn't any monster at all. It was just Mummy putting the dishes away but she must have forgotten where they stayed and she had put them all away in the wrong place. Evie giggled to herself.

She was so glad it had only been the two of them for dinner last night or her little legs would have been very tired carrying all the pots and pans, all the knives and forks and all the plates and cups back down to the kitchen.

Evie gingerly got out of bed as she didn't want to smash anything, and as she did, she thought how much she loved her mummy and wondered what they would be doing that day. Evie thought her mummy would probably be busy in the kitchen cooking the lovely sizzling bacon or wrapping Christmas presents like she did every year. Evie sniffed the air and wondered why she could not smell the delicious aroma of sizzling bacon floating up the stairs to her. She took a great big sniff and wiggled her little nose. No! She definitely could not smell sizzling bacon.

Evie suddenly thought of the monster again and wondered if he had eaten all the bacon but then she gave a little giggle and told herself not to be so silly.

Of course, there was no monster and of course, the monster had not eaten her lovely sizzling bacon, but then

Evie wondered why if the monster had not eaten the lovely sizzling bacon, she could not smell it and she felt a little bit sad.

Evie had always loved waking up to the smell of sizzling bacon wafting up the stairs. Evie's mummy had always spoiled her on Sundays and school holidays with a lovely cooked breakfast. The smell had always made her want to bound out of bed and rush down the stairs, so with a disappointed look on her little face and a rumbling tummy, Evie decided that she would go and see what Mummy was doing. Evie thought that maybe they would be going shopping for presents and the thoughts of monsters and of the lovely sizzling bacon was soon forgotten.

Evie bounded down the stairs in her usual two at a time way, that her mummy had always shouted at her for doing but this morning she was just too excited to think about that. Evie ran into her mummy's lovely bright red kitchen. Evie's mum never used to like bright colours but now she loved them.

She had told Evie that it cheered her up and made seeing things easier for her as her eyesight was not as good as it used to be. Evie found her mummy searching all the cupboards shaking her head and tutting to herself.

Evie suddenly remembered all the pots and pans, all the knives and forks and all the plates and cups were still sitting on her little bed so Evie charged back upstairs and brought down all the pots and pans, all the knives and forks and all the plates and cups. Evie's mummy looked at Evie in surprise and asked where on earth she had found them?

So Evie explained that she had woken up and felt something heavy on her bed and had thought it was a big scary monster who had eaten all the lovely sizzling bacon until she peeped over the top of her duvet and realised it was just dishes. Evie's mummy said, "You do know there is no such thing as monsters and there is definitely no such thing as guzzling, sizzling-bacon-eating monsters, don't you, Evie?"

Evie and her mummy laughed out loud so hard until they were bent over holding their tummies and their faces started to hurt. Evie suddenly noticed that although her mummy was laughing hard, she also looked excited and wondered what her mummy was up to, Evie guessed her mummy must have a surprise for her.

Evie could always tell when her mummy was up to something as she was a smart child; her teachers had told her so.

Evie ran up to her mummy, tilted her little head back and with an inquisitive look on her little face she looked up at her mummy and asked what the surprise was? Evie's mummy laughed and said, "Oh, little Evie, you know me so well, go and look out of the window."

Evie ran to the window, threw the curtains back and squealed in delight. It was snowing. Great big giant flakes of lovely, white, fluffy snow. Evie loved the snow and could not contain her excitement. She danced around and around her mummy, singing 'it's snowing, it's snowing'.

This was making Evie's mummy even more dizzy than she

normal was and Evie's mummy could stand it no longer, so laughingly she grabbed Evie's hands and said, "Calm down, Evie, or you will have no energy left to go to the park." Evie gave another squeal of delight and ran back to the window to make sure the snow had not stopped.

The snow was coming down fast but Evie still worried it would stop and they would not be able to go to the park after all, so she gulped her breakfast cereal down as quickly as she could and tried not to think of the lovely, sizzling bacon that she had tucked into every other Christmas eve morning.

Evie knew it was not her mummy's fault that she could not cook any more. Evie's mummy had told her it was too dangerous for her to use the oven now as she might forget she was cooking or forget to turn the cooker off.

With all her silly thoughts of monsters swamping her head that morning, Evie had totally forgotten her mummy could not cook anymore and Evie felt a little bit guilty for forgetting. So, Evie gave her mummy a great, big, tight bear hug and then bounced back up the stairs to get some warm clothes on.

Evie did not see her mummy standing by the window looking at her with a huge smile on her face. She loved her little daughter so much and her heart would break a little every time she wondered what her little daughter would look like when she grew up, or what Evie's little children would look like.

But today was not a day to worry or ponder on such things;

today was going to be a happy memorable day. Evie's mummy was determined to fill her little daughter's life with memories and special moments and this Christmas was goingto be filled with fun, laughter and happiness even if there was no lovely, crispy, sizzling bacon. Evie was at last ready to go.

She was dressed in her new pink spotted coat, her red Wellington boots and her white fluffy hat, gloves and scarf. Evie's mummy laughed and said she looked as snug as a bug in a rug.

Evie joined in and laughed with her mummy but then Evie noticed her mummy was still not ready. Evie's mummy only had one boot on.

Evie's mummy smiled. She circled her bare foot around and around and as she did, she wiggled her toes in the air and asked Evie if she would like to play their special game?

The game today was going to be called 'hunt the boot'. Evie clapped her hands and danced on the spot with excitement saying, "Yes, please, Mummy, let's play. Can we start the game now?" Evie loved this game. Evie and Evie's mummy played it often and it was always such fun because Evie's mummy was very good at it.

Evie's mummy always found unusual, exciting places to hide things for Evie to find. Evie began by searching the kitchen cupboards, then she searched in the fridge but no the boot was not there. Once Mummy had hidden her hat in the bin so she searched there too, but no, the boot was not there. Evie searched the bright red cooker but no, the boot was not there either.

Evie wondered where to search next? They had to find Mummy's boot or they would not be able to go to the park.

Evie's mummy could not go out with one boot on and one boot off. Everyone would laugh and point at her and Evie did not like it when other people laughed at her mummy. It always made her angry and then she would cry.

She always tried so hard not to, but the tears always came. Evie just wished that people would understand that her mummy could not help being the way she was and sometimes she just did not remember things, but she was still a person with a huge heart, feelings and a wonderful sense of humour.

Most importantly, she was her mummy and she loved her mummy more than anything or anyone in the whole wide world. Evie suddenly remembered the lost boot and laughingly noted to herself that everyone forgets things now and then; even she did. Evie smiled and thought to herself, Where could the missing boot be? Evie put her finger up to her lips and thought hard, Where could the boot be? She wondered. She bounded up the stairs again and looked in Mummy's bedroom.

She searched the cupboards and even in the drawers but no, the boot was not there. She looked under the bed, on top of the wardrobes in the laundry basket, but no, the boot was not there either.

She looked in the hot press and in the spare room but no the boot was not there. Next, Evie searched her own bedroom, in her wardrobes and even amongst all her teddy bears but no, the boot was not there, so she looked in the bathroom and there in plain view, right in front of her very own nose was Mummy's missing boot. Mummy had hidden her boot in the sink.

Evie giggled at the thought of her mummy hiding her boot in the sink and she shouted down, "I found it," Evie thought to herself how brilliant her mummy was. Her mummy was so good at this game; she was way better than her friends' mums or dads, and she loved playing the game as it was such fun.

At last Evie's mummy was ready and the missing boot was securely attached on to Evie's mummy's foot. The only thing they had to do now was fix Mummy's coat as Evie's mummy had buttoned it up wrong. Evie knew that her mummy could no longer cook her lovely sizzling bacon and sometimes forgot where she left things but Evie also knew that her mummy still liked to be as independent as possible.

So instead of Evie fixing her mummies coat for her, Evie rubbed her little tummy, tapped her head and hopped on one foot and asked her mummy if she could do it too.

Evie's mummy laughed and rubbed her tummy, tapped her head and hopped on one foot. As she did this, she noticed her coat was buttoned wrong. Evie's mummy said, "Oh dear me, Evie! Look at my coat. What a state I look … I meant to fix that but I totally forgot all about it." Evie and her mummy giggled as Evie's mummy buttoned up her coat properly, and Evie secretly thought to herself how proud she was of her mummy.

On the way to the park, Evie skipped happily along, singing her favourite song and holding her mummy's hand. Evie and her mummy always held hands as Evie's mummy said Evie was so young that it was not safe for her to run on by herself and Evie knew her mummy could not walk very well. Sometimes, her mummy would forget where she was going and get lost, so they had both agreed to help each other and keep each other safe. Evie thought how lucky they were that the park was close to their home and there was only one road to cross. Evie was glad it had traffic lights as that made it easier to cross over.

Evie always worried about her mummy crossing roads as she could not see or hear very well and sometimes, she would forget to check that the light was green for them. So Evie held her mummy's hand even tighter and waited until it was safe for them to cross the road.

Before going into the park, Evie's mummy said she had a treat for them both. Evie looked up at her mummy with pleasant surprise and asked her mummy what it was?

Evie's mummy said, "I will give you a clue; it is something that will warm up your hands." Evie looked confused; she thought her mummy had forgotten she had her gloves on so she held up her hands and waved them so her mummy could see. Evie's mummy laughed and said, "No, it's not gloves. I will give you another clue …

can you smell anything nice?"

Evie sniffed the air and did a little happy dance. She could smell the lovely aroma of sizzling bacon wafting all around her. Evie clapped her hands in delight.

Evie's mummy said they were going to the café as she could not have her little daughter going without her sizzling bacon on Christmas eve. Evie smiled and thanked her mummy as they both hurried into the café.

Evie and her mummy both ordered sausage, egg and sizzling bacon baps. Evie's mouth watered as she held the warm bap in both of her little hands.

Evie decided to keep her lovely bap until they reached the park so she could sit down and savour every delicious mouthful. As Evie and her mummy entered the park, Evie squealed in delight. The snow was deep and Evie sank down into it; it was so deep that the tops of her boots were covered and she laughed and asked her mummy where her boots had gone? Evie's mummy said, "I don't know, Evie but I definitely hope they are not in the sink with mine."

Evie and her mummy both giggled at this. Then Evie's mummy said, "Come on, Evie, lets catch some snow with our tongues."

Evie loved this idea and Evie and her mummy ran around and around the park with their tongues sticking out catching the little snowflakes. Evie could not help giggling.

She was sure they must have looked really silly running around with their tongues hanging out but she didn't care. She was having fun and the snow was lovely and light; on her tongue.

Evie and her mummy played this game until they were both exhausted and fell into the snow laughing. Evie's mummy asked Evie if she wanted to eat her sizzling bacon bap or whether she wanted to build a snowman next?

Evie was having so much fun with her mummy that she had forgotten all about her lovely sizzling bacon bap, and she didn't want to stop to eat it now. Evie was too excited to think about food even if it was lovely, sizzling bacon. Evie wanted to build a big, huge snowman.

Evie giggled clapped her hands and said, "Yes, please, Mummy! Let's build a great, big snowman." Evie's mummy smiled and said she would build the snowman's body and Evie could build the head so Evie and her mummy made a snowball each.

Then they started to roll them along in the snow and the snow balls grew bigger and bigger and bigger until they were so big that Evie could not move hers.

So, Evie's mummy rolled them together and they lifted the

head on to the body but as they did, the top of the snowman's head fell off and landed back in the snow right at their feet. Evie and her mummy laughed and Evie's mummy said they would have to fix him as they could not leave poor Mr Snowman with half a head.

Evie said Mr Snowman could wear his hat and then it would not matter but Evie's mummy told Evie that Mr Snowman needed all his head because that was where his brain should be.

Evie looked at her mummy with a questioning, thoughtful expression on her face, then slowly a big smile spread across her face. "Of course, Mummy, you are right!" How would the snowman think or move or feel or do anything without a brain? Everyone knows it is your brain that controls everything your body can do; even your thoughts and feelings.

Evie looked at Mr Snowman and thought he looked very sad without all of his head so Evie and her mummy got more snow and started to pack it to the rest of Mr Snowman's head.

Soon he had a lovely, round, smooth head that Evie and her mummy were pleased with. All he needed now was two eyes, a nose and a mouth.

Evie had brought two eyes with her from one of her old dolls, a big bendy carrot for his nose, and for his mouth she had brought red jellybeans thinking if they had too many, she could eat the leftovers. Evie's mummy told her she was a clever girl to think of those items and Evie was pleased she had thought ahead. Evie had even brought an old orange shirt and a brown suit with the buttons missing. She wanted to make Mr Snowman perfect; all she needed now was two long sticks so Mr Snowman would have arms.

When Evie had finished, she stood back with her hands on her hips and looked at the friendly snowman they had built.

Evie thought Mr Snowman was wonderful and asked her mummy, if she thought Mr Snowman would be safe in the park on his own all night? Evie thought he might be scared or lonely and she didn't want him to be sad.

Evie wanted to take him home and give him some lovely, hot, sizzling bacon. Evie still had a worried look on her little face so Evie's mummy reminded Evie that although they had given Mr Snowman a head, he still did not have a brain.

Without a brain he could not move or think or feel any emotions so he would not be lonely or sad. Evie considered this and looked at Mr Snowman. She wanted so badly to believe that Mr Snowman could feel and hear and see just like she could but she knew her mummy was telling the truth and without a brain those things were just not possible. Just at that moment, the biggest snow flake Evie had ever seen, landed right on the tip of her nose. It was very cold and Evie giggled and wriggled her nose so the snowflake would slide down into her waiting, open mouth but the snow flake broke and started to melt.

Evie's mummy looked up and asked Evie to look at all the little snowflakes gently floating down to the ground. Evie's mummy asked her what she saw and Evie replied, "Lots of pretty little snowflakes." Evie's mummy said she was right; there were indeed lots of pretty, little snowflakes but did Evie know that all the little snowflakes where different?

That in fact, there was never two little snowflakes ever the same. Evie was surprised as they all looked the same to her but Evie's mummy said that actually they are all unique, and as the little snowflakes float down to earth, they develop and change and some get bigger; their patterns also change and sometimes they even get damaged.

Evie thought about this and remembered building Mr Snowman and all the paths his head had left in the snow.

Evie thought the paths looked like a maze and with an inquisitive look on her little face Evie asked her mummy if that was the same? Evie's mummy laughed and said, "Yes, Evie, you are a very clever girl.

It is the same." Rolling the snowman's head along in the snow had made the snowman's head get bigger and bigger; it had even caused his head to get damaged.

"Travelling those paths is called a journey and just like the little snowflakes and the snow balls, people's lives are also a journey.

So you see Evie … if you look carefully, you will see the snowflakes are not all the same; just as people are not all the same. Everyone has a brain that looks the same

but just like the little snowflakes, on closer inspection, you will see that every brain is actually unique."

Evie had a puzzled look on her little face and asked her mummy how every brain was different but they looked the same, so Evie's mummy explained that everyone's brain structure is made up of two things; the first thing is genetic factors and the second is life experiences so it is very unlikely that two different people will have the same genetics and take the exact same journey through life.

Evie pondered on what her mummy had said as they started to walk home hand in hand. She turned to wave goodbye to Mr Snowman; he looked so alone and lost in the middle of the park all by himself.

Evie hated leaving him all on his own. She wanted so much to be able to take him home and share all of the lovely sizzling bacon with him, but she knew she couldn't as Mr Snowman didn't have a brain.

So, he could not walk, think, taste or feel, without a brain. Mr Snowman was incapable of doing anything so Evie ran back and threw her little arms tightly round his neck and whispered into his ear that she would come back and visit him again soon. Evie ran back to her mummy.

She was so glad her mummy had a brain even though Evie knew her mummy could sometimes not remember things and that part of her mummy's brain had become injured through illness. Evie was so pleased that her mummy could still be happy and laugh and cry and walk and talk. She had her mummy to love her and care for her. Evie knew she was not alone as Evie and her mummy had each other.

Thinking of this made Evie feel very sad for Mr Snowman. It had been such a lovely day but leaving Mr Snowman all alone made Evie want to cry and a little tear ran down her cheek. Evie put her hand in her pocket to get her tissue and as she did, she felt a little package.

As Evie felt the little package, she suddenly remembered she had magic dust. Evie had always worried Santa would not be able to get down the chimney, so her mummy always bought her magic dust so Santa would fit down the chimney later that night.

Evie looked at the little parcel and felt excited; she had butterflies in her tummy, as she held the dust tightly in her hand. Evie thought if she used the magic dust now it would be worth not getting any presents; if only the magic dust could make the snowman come to life.

Evie closed her eyes tightly and from the bottom of her heart she made her wish, then she circled around and around and around.

Evie opened her hand and let the magic dust float up into the air. Just then, a very dark cloud appeared and big drops of rain began to fall, and as this happened all of the magic dust fell down onto the lovely, white snowflakes right at Evie's little feet. Evie looked down and became very sad as she thought all her efforts had been for nothing and she had wasted all the magic dust so she began to cry.

Evie's mummy picked up her little daughter and cuddled her tight. She didn't like seeing her little daughter so sad. As she did this, a sudden gust of wind came and blew off Evie's mummy's big blue hat; the wind was so strong it pushed Evie and her mummy down into the snow.Evie's mummy had never known a wind to be so strong;

the wind seemed to be swirling around them Evie and her mummy could not get up as every time they tried, the wind pushed them down again. Evie's mummy started to get very worried. The wind was so strong it was frightening.

All she could do to protect her little daughter was to shelter little Evie inside her big, warm, winter coat. She covered Evie's little head and hoped the wind would go away so they could get home before dark but Evie started to wriggle and giggle. Evie was squirming so much that Evie's mummy could not keep her coat around her to protect her from the wind.

When Evie's mummy looked down at Evie, she noticed that Evie was actually laughing. Evie's mummy wondered what on earth Evie could possibly find so funny? Evie's mummy looked at her with a very confused expression on her face and started to wonder if her brain was playing tricks on her again and if she was hallucinating?

Suddenly Evie's mummy felt something on her side. She was just about to brush it off when it began tickling her. Evie's mummy could not stop herself laughing; the tickle was so light and feathery. Soon Evie and her mummy were laughing so much that they had tears running down their faces.

Neither of them could understand what was tickling them until Evie could stand no more and cried out, "Stop! Please stop ... Please, please stop!" Evie and her mummy had been so busy laughing that they had not noticed lots of snowflakes swirling all around them or that Mr Snowman, the baps, the eggs, the sausages and the lovely sizzling bacon strips were all running around the park waving their arms in the air and laughing uncontrollably.

Mr Snowman looked at Evie and shouted, "Look at me everyone! I have a brain now ... look I can move my legs, I can wave my arms, I can even laugh and I can cry." Evie's mummy looked shocked but Evie was thrilled and excited so she waved back to Mr Snowman, the baps, the eggs, the sausages and the lovely sizzling bacon strips. Suddenly, a little voice behind them popped up and startled them both. Evie and her mummy gasped. The tiny little snowflake had the biggest, brightest, blue eyes and kindest face Evie and her mummy had ever seen. Evie's mummy was still sitting in shock. She knew this could not be real and wondered if she was indeed having a hallucination?

Evie's mummy rubbed her eyes and blinked several times but the snow flake was still there.

Evie's mummy wondered if she was imagining the little

snow flake just like Evie had imagined the ugly monster on her bed that morning, so she shook her head vigorously from side to side, over and over again then looked in disbelief as the little snowflake was still standing there right in front of her.

So, Evie's mummy then pinched herself. She squeezed her eyes tightly shut and counted to ten, but no, she wasn't imagining or dreaming or hallucinating this time; her brain wasn't playing tricks on her. The pretty little snowflake was still standing there right in front of her very own eyes and the little snowflake was smiling at her.

Evie's mummy asked the little snowflake how this could be? How could snowflakes, snowmen, bacon and baps, eggs and sausages all come to life? The little white snowflake called Daisy smiled and said, "Evie wished with all her heart that she could be in a land where everyone and everything, even snowmen, sausages, bacon, eggs and baps would have a brain and could live; the magic dust blew and now we are all in this wonderful land that Evie wished for."

Evie jumped up and clapped her hands in glee. She was so excited Mr Snowman had a brain and was able to run, walk, think, feel, play, talk and most importantly laugh. Evie hugged Mr Snowman and they danced together.Evie looked on in delight as Sizzling bacon with his long dangly legs did a wibble-wobble dance. The flat eggs

joined in flipping and flopping, the long sausages twisted and turned and the round fat baps bobbed and bounced all over the park. Evie giggled! She could not believe the spectacle she was seeing right in front of her very own eyes. Evie was very glad that she had not eaten the sizzling bacon, the baps, the sausages or the eggs as now Mr Snowman would have some friends and would not be lonely.

As Evie watched Mr Snowman, the Sizzling bacon, the baps, the sausages and the eggs having lots of fun, all the little snowflakes started to float in circles around her. Evie was gently being lifted up and twirled around.

The little snowflakes and Evie were all dancing together; around and around Evie went with the snowflakes. The little snowflakes floated around her tickling Evie's little button nose as Evie hummed a tune for them all to dance to; they were all so happy.

Evie was laughing so much, her little tummy and her face hurt. Evie suddenly realised her mummy was not dancing with them.

She looked around and saw her mummy still sitting in the wet snow. Evie's little heart plummeted; she thought her mummy looked very alone and very sad.

Evie didn't want her mummy to be alone or sad so she called out for her mummy to join them. Evie was having so much fun and she wanted her mummy to dance too, but Evie's mummy reminded Evie that she couldn't.

Evie had forgotten that her mummy could not dance any more as she could not remember the steps or the words to most songs. Evie felt a little guilty that she had forgotten again and she didn't like reminding her mummy of the things she couldn't do.

Instead, she liked to remind her mummy of the things she could still do. A little snowflake who had huge, green, kind eyes and very large ears who was still sitting beside Evie's mummy jumped up and looked Evie's mummy straight in the eye.

Studying her the little snowflake eventually smiled and said, "I am Twinkie ... why you are worried that you won't be able to dance?" Evie's mummy looked at Twinkie, said hello and shook his tiny hand very carefully. Then she told him that she wanted to dance and have fun so badly but she knew she couldn't, because she was ill, her brain did not work properly now and because of this she had forgotten more and more over time.

Twinkie didn't understand and asked Evie's mummy, what a brain was? Evie's mummy could not help herself from smiling at the little snowflake; he was so cute and inquisitive.

Evie's mummy said, "Well, Mr Twinkie, a brain is found inside your head and your brain is made up of different sections and without your brain you would not be able to live."

Twinkie looked shocked at this. He studied Evie's mummy very intently and then asked, why her brain didn't work right?

Evie's mummy told Twinkie that her brain used to work right and that she was actually very intelligent but she had got an illness that is called dementia and that is what had damaged her brain.

Twinkie looked confused. He thought dementia must be a great big, evil, green monster and very cruel to have hurt

Evie's lovely mummy in this way. Twinkie quickly jumped up startling Evie's mummy and tightly clenched his little fists. He told Evie's mummy in a very strong powerful voice that he was going to hunt down the horrible, nasty, beast and fight him to he very end.

Twinkie imagined he could see the nasty beast in front of him. He told Evie's mummy that he wished he had a huge sword so he could kill the evil beast. Evie's mummy looked at Twinkie in amusement as Twinkie punched and punched and kicked and kicked the air until he was finally exhausted and fell flat out on his back in the snow gasping for breath.

Twinkie felt really sad for Evie's mummy so he called all the other snowflakes together and announced that they had a great, big, evil beast called dementia to slay. Twinkie told the others that dementia was a nasty beast that had made Evie's mummy ill by damaging her brain, and because of that they would all go to war to destroy the horrible, nasty, ugly beast. all the other little snowflakes cheered and began to file up into rows like a little army getting ready to go into battle,

Evie's mummy looked at Twinkie with amusement in her eyes she knew Twinkie and the other little snowflakes did not understand but she was pleased that they all cared and wanted to help her so Evie's mummy explained to everyone that although sadly, dementia is cruel, it unfortunately is not a live beast so it cannot be slayed.

Evie's mummy told all the little snowflakes that she wished dementia was just a cruel, ugly, beast and could be easily defeated but sadly that was the not case. Evie's mummy explained that dementia is caused when the brain becomes damaged due to injury or illness through

your lifetime.

She told Twinkie that there are lots of different types of dementia and in fact there are over two hundred different types; and that the two most common are Alzheimer's and vascular dementia and which symptoms you have depends on which dementia you have and which part of the brain is damaged.

Twinkie looked very confused. He didn't understand so Evie's mummy explained that different parts of your brain control different functions within your body and that the parts of her brain that were damaged controlled her memory, her thinking process, and her movements and that was why she could not remember very well and had problems walking.

Sizzling bacon who had been listening intently to Evie's mummy, suddenly jumped to his feet and proceeded to fall flat on his face in the snow with his arms and legs spread

out; his little body was almost covered in
the cold, wet snow.

Sizzling bacon turned his brown, crispy head and asked in a sorrow full little voice if he also had dementia. Evie's mummy looked at Sizzle in surprise and asked Sizzle why he would think such a thing?

Sizzling bacon explained that now he had a brain but his legs didn't work right and he kept falling flat on his face. Evie's mummy gave a hearty laugh and said, "Ohh, little Sizzle, you have no need to worry about your brain ... it is working very well; your only problem is your legs are so long and dangly, you have only gotten your brain and it will take a bit of practice for your brain and legs to coordinate for your legs to work properly." Sizzling bacon gave a huge sigh of relief and even though he was still lying face down in the snow, he wiped the nervous sweat off his little brow.

After feeling scared in this manner Sizzling bacon was even more interested in how his brain worked; he was fascinated with the idea that something inside his head that he could not see, hold or feel could control all his other bodily organs and everything he did or thought.

With an inquisitive look on his brown crispy face, Sizzling bacon asked if dementia could cause Evie's mummy to get any other symptoms. Evie's mummy told Sizzling bacon that she hoped not but sadly if more of her brain became damaged then she would indeed get more symptoms.

Evie's mummy explained that sometimes dementia affected

your eyesight or you were more prone to infections; normal daily activities such as bathing or eating become harder as it becomes more difficult for your brain to process the thoughts required to complete the activities.

Evie's mummy then told Sizzling bacon that sometimes dementia can even affect your emotions making you feel sad or scared and some people can also have problems controlling their temper.

Sizzling bacon looked startled at this and started to crawl away on his hands and knees as fast as his dangly arms and legs would allow him through the cold wet snow.

Sizzling bacon looked at Evie's mummy out of the corner of his eye. He could not imagine Evie's mummy losing her temper and shouting at anyone or worse still hitting them; she looked so kind and gentle.

He was so angry with dementia for doing this and a little tear ran down his brown crispy face.

Evie's mummy knew Sizzle was scared and sad so she took his tiny brown hand in hers and reassured Sizzle that her mood would only be affected if that part of her brain became damaged, and at the moment that part of her brain was perfectly healthy.

Sizzling bacon was so relieved he wriggled in the snow, then got to his feet to do a little happy dance but fell right back down on his face in the snow once again. "Ohh dear!" said Evie's mummy. Twinkie and Evie's mummy took Sizzling bacon by the hands and told Sizzling bacon not to worry as they would help him to walk and run and do his funny little dance without falling flat on his face.

Sizzling bacon was very grateful to be offered help; he didn't know how Evie's mummy coped all day, every day with her brain not working properly. He had only thought his brain didn't work right and he was distraught at the thought, so he wrapped his brown, dangly, crispy arms around Evie's mummy's neck tightly in a great big bear hug and told Evie's mummy that he was very proud of her for staying strong and fighting the nasty dementia. Evie's mummy hugged Sizzling bacon back and said, "Thank you, Sizzle, but I am not the only strong one; little Evie is just as strong and she is only ten years old." Sizzling bacon looked confused again and asked how could little Evie be just as strong as Evie's mummy, as Evie wasn't fighting the nasty beast, dementia?

Evie's mummy looked into Sizzling bacon's crispy, brown face and with a sad little smile on her own face she told Sizzling bacon that dementia was a battle that they were both fighting and they fought it together every single day of life.

Evie's mummy explained that even though she was the one who had the symptoms of dementia, it was equally difficult for little Evie to watch her mummy deteriorating slowly over time and it was even more difficult because there was no one else to help Evie or Evie's mummy.

Evie's mummy told Twinkie and Sizzling bacon that Evie had to help her mummy with all the things every other mother did on a daily basis without even thinking about it and because of this little Evie was missing out on part of her childhood. Sizzling bacon looked very thoughtful considering the position Evie and Evie's mummy were in.

Twinkie and Sizzling bacon both felt sad that Evie's mummy was ill, but they felt equally sad that little Evie could not go out with her friends any time she wanted or play leisurely on the swings or go swimming just when she fancied it. And with a tiny little voice they both said, "We agree with you. It must be very difficult for you both." Evie's mummy nodded and explained to Sizzling bacon and Twinkie that they had both talked about it and agreed that as long as they were both coping and they were both still happy, they would continue to help each other as they loved each other very much.

Evie's mummy told Sizzling bacon and Twinkie that she thought Evie was very strong and she was very proud of her little daughter, so she tried to make Evie's life as happy as possible and fill it with as much joy and laughter as she could possibly squeeze in.

She told Sizzling bacon and Twinkie that little Evie was in fact, a young carer but she didn't want little Evie to be a young carer; she wanted Evie to be a child and have childhood memories and she was doing her best to make that happen.

Sizzling bacon started to cry again. He felt so sorry for little Evie and now he realised that, yes indeed, little Evie was in fact just as strong as her mummy. Sizzling bacon felt his little crispy heart swell with pride for both of them.

Evie's mummy told Sizzling bacon how that morning she had lost her boot, buttoned her coat wrong, left all the dinner dishes on Evie's bed causing her to think a big, scary monster was on her bed with her.

Sizzling bacon's eyes popped wide open and he asked if the scary monster was still there, waiting for them?

Sizzling bacon said he was too scared to fight the monster himself but he knew the snowflakes would help if they asked them to.

Evie's mummy clapped her hand over her mouth and giggled making Sizzling bacon's crispy, brown face turn bright red as he looked down at his feet in embarrassment. Evie's mummy told Sizzling bacon not to be embarrassed and that there was no big, scary monster; it had just been the dishes she had left there by mistake and to top the day off, there had been no sizzling bacon to eat either.

At this, Sizzling bacon's eyes widened until Evie's mummy thought they were going to pop right out of his tiny, crispy, brown head. Stuttering, Sizzling bacon asked if they were actually going to eat him? Evie's mummy laughed and reassured Sizzling bacon that they couldn't eat him as she wasn't able to cook anymore.

Twinkie thought about all he had listened to and he was astonished. Twinkie had no idea that your brain did all that work, but he still looked very sad when he thought of little Evie and Evie's mummy. He sat very quietly staring into space with a very pensive look on his face.

Twinkie had a very important question in his head that he wanted to ask but he didn't want to upset Evie's mummy.

Twinkie thought about it some more and then he decided it was best to ask rather than worry about it, so in a very quiet voice Twinkie asked Evie's mummy, if everyone gets dementia? Sizzling bacon looked startled at this question.

He hadn't contemplated that little Evie could possibly get dementia too and the thought frightened him so much that he raised his little, crispy, brown fist and shook it in

Twinkie's face, shouting at him not to be so stupid.

Evie's mummy watched the little outburst and decided she had better jump in and answer before they started fighting and one of them got hurt. So, Evie's mummy gently lifted Sizzling bacon in one hand and Twinkie in the other hand and told them there was no need to fight and to apologise to each other.

Evie's mummy could not help smiling as the two little arms reached out and Sizzling bacon and Twinkie shook hands mumbling their apologies to each other at the same time.

Evie's mummy giggled at the cuteness of the two of them but then she remembered the question and took on a serious tone and said, "Sometimes dementia can run in families but in most cases, dementia is not inherited; most dementias do not run down through families. In fact, it's quite rare for that to happen."

Sizzling bacon and Twinkie looked very worried and asked Evie's mummy which dementia

she had? Evie's mummy said, "I have vascular dementia and to answer your first question, it's a very big 'NO'!" Evie's mummy shook her head from side to side and stated quite loudly, "No, definitely not! Everyone does not get dementia and hopefully Evie will never get it either."

Sizzling bacon and Twinkie let out loud sighs of relief and gave Evie's mummy huge big smiles. To reassure them both, Evie's mummy explained to Twinkie and Sizzling

bacon that dementia was mostly an older person's illness, but some younger people like herself could also get young onset dementia if their brain became damaged through illness or injury.

Twinkie put his hands on his hips, tilted his head and thought about everything Evie's mummy had said. He felt sad for Evie and her mummy and asked Evie's mummy, what it was like when her brain didn't work the way it was supposed to? Evie's mummy gave a sad little smile and told Twinkie and Sizzling bacon that it was not very nice, and that some people laughed at her and thought she was stupid; whereas in reality she was a highly intelligent person and people just thought she was stupid because her brain had just stopped working properly, and sometimes she could not remember even simple things or simple words.

Evie's mummy told Twinkie and Sizzling bacon that some people were even scared of her, as they thought they could catch dementia from her.

Evie's mummy laughed to herself at this and told Twinkie how ridiculous that was as you could not catch dementia from someone else but it always made her feel sad when peoplethought that way.

Twinkie shook his head from side to side and looked very sad for Evie's mummy. He asked Evie's mummy if she would get better?

Evie's mummy shook her head and said no, she would not get better unless someone found a cure. Evie's mummy didn't like people to be sad when they thought

of her, as Evie's mummy wanted to enjoy her life and have as much fun as she could. So she answered quickly telling

Twinkie as there was no cure, that she might eventually get worse and might not be able to remember who her family or friends were, or where she lived; and that she might eventually forget almost everything. Twinkie began to cry and looked so sad. He could not help thinking how horrible that stupid, evil beast dementia was.

Twinkie shouted at the top of his little voice, "Go away dementia! Go away and get lost and never ever come back. You're stupid and I hate you!" Twinkie stamped his little feet in frustration as there was nothing he could do to cure Evie's mummy.

He looked so sad that Sizzling bacon put his thin, crispy, brown arm around his new friend and gave him a great, big hug. Evie's mummy looked at Twinkie and her heart strings pulled. She told Twinkie that dementia or not she wanted to live her life and be happy; that she wanted to have fun and laugh and cry and make memories.

Evie's mummy didn't want Twinkie to be sad or feel sorry for her so she explained again that how bad her memory would get, would all depend on how much of her brain became damaged, and that she was staying positive that her illness would not get any worse.

Then Evie's mummy gave Twinkie a great big smile and told Twinkie and Sizzling bacon that she sometimes forgets Evie's name and she calls her Effie instead. Twinkie and Sizzling bacon did not see what was funny about that and looked confused until Evie's mummy explained that Effie was their pet dog's name.Then Twinkie, Sizzling bacon and Evie's mummy all burst into fits of giggles.

Twinkie reached out his tiny arm and told Evie's mum to take his hand. Evie's mummy shook her head and said no, she was scared to take Twinkie's hand in case she hurt him.

Twinkie looked to his friends and called for them to come and help Evie's mummy. Quickly, Evie's mummy was surrounded in tiny, white snowflakes. Twinkie asked Sizzling bacon to take Evie's mummy's hand and then Twinkie shouted to Bracken, as he was the biggest snowflake of them all to take Evie's mummy's other hand and help her.

Bracken smiled at Evie's mum, titled his tiny green hat at her and floated down to take Evie's mummy's other hand. Evie's mummy felt herself slowly rising up from the cold, wet ground.

Evie's mummy was floating; the little snowflakes flew all around her gently floating past, lightly tickling her until she had to laugh. Evie's mummy was delighted; it was such a thrilling, wonderful feeling to be able

to dance again.

Evie was on cloud nine to see her mummy so happy. Evie asked the little snowflake beside her who wore a bright red dress and a huge yellow hat, how could that be, as Evie knew her mummy's brain did notwork properly? Daisy laughed and said, "Evie, you wished for a land where everything and everyone has a perfect brain and is alive so here your mummy does not have dementia." Evie was thrilled. Her wish had made her mummy better. She laughed and danced with her mummy wishing with all her heart that they could stay like this forever.

Daisy floated around until she dropped down onto Evie's mummy's nose making Evie's mummy sneeze and sneeze and sneeze.

Poor Daisy was nearly blown away and had to hold on tight to Evie's mummy's eyelashes. Her little feet were trying desperately to get a foot hold on Evie's mummy's cheek but they kept slipping off.

Bracken didn't want Daisy to be blown away so he balanced right on the tip of Evie's mummy's nose and held on tight to Daisy's hand, while Sizzling bacon lay across Evie's mummy's face grabbing one ear with his hands and her other ear with his feet making himself into a barrier to stop Daisy or Bracken from falling.

After Evie's mummy eventually stopped sneezing, and there was no chance of daisy being blown away, Daisy hugged Bracken and Sizzling bacon and said 'thank you' to both of them and she hopped Evie's mummy didn't sneeze again.

They all laughed and Bracken announced that Daisy was welcome as everyone needs a helping hand at times.

Daisy was glad she hadn't got blown away so she shook and twisted and danced on Evie's mummy's nose so hard that Evie and her mummy burst out laughing.

They could not help it. Daisy looked so comical. They were all so happy and having such fun that Evie's mummy started to sing a song; the words just came out of her mouth—her brain was working again.

She was so surprised that she could actually remember

the words now and even the dance steps. It was so exhilarating; she felt her cheeks flushing and her heart beat started to race.

She felt light and free and her feet just would not stop moving, Evie was thrilled her little face shone with pride and happiness.

She was dancing with her mummy; around and around they all went laughing and crying with tears of joy streaming down their cheeks because they were all just so happy.

But then Evie's mummy noticed it was dark. She did not want to stop dancing but she knew they had to return home.

Evie's mummy wanted to stay in the park where she could dance and sing and not have dementia, but she knew she had to go home and the dementia would return and so would the forgetfulness, as dementia or not it was her home and she would miss her life if she stayed here. Evie didn't want to go either.

She wanted to stay with Mr Snowman, Sizzling bacon, Daisy, Bracken, Twinkie and all the other snowflakes. She looked at Mr Snowman with a sorrowful expression on her little face and asked if she and her mummy could stay.

Mr Snowman knelt down on one knee, lifted Evie onto his lap and cuddled her. Evie was getting cold and wet and she began to shiver but she didn't mind.

She felt safe with Mr Snowman. Mr Snowman said she could stay but would she not miss her family and friends?

Evie thought and nodded her little head, "Yes," she replied, "I would miss them all, so instead of staying here can I visit you?" Daisy, Brackon, Twinkie, Sizzling bacon, Mr Snowman and all the others nodded and said, "Yes of course, you can!" Mr Snowman took Evie's little finger in his own and pinkie promised Evie that they would all see each other again very soon. Evie smiled at Mr Snowman and gave him a huge, big, tight, 'bear hug goodbye'.

Evie and her mummy held hands and walked slowly towards the park gates waving goodbye to their new friends. As they got closer to the gate, a cold wet mist enclosed them.

Evie and her mummy could hardly see Mr Snowman, Sizzling bacon or the little snowflakes now, and their hearts saddened a little more. Evie's mummy couldn't remember where the park gate was; she was very confused and started to walk in the wrong direction.

Evie noticed that her mummy was going in the wrong direction and asked her mummy if her brain wasn't working right again? Evie's mummy sighed and nodded and said, "Yes, little Evie, the dementia is back," so Evie squeezed her mummy's hand tightly in her own little hand and lead her mummy safely out of the park.

Evie loved her mummy, dementia or not, monsters on the bed or not, sizzling bacon or not. Her mummy would always be her mummy, and even if her mummy did not have a very good memory and didn't remember her in the future, she knew in her little heart that she would always know and love her mummy.

Evie suddenly had a brilliant idea. She skipped along excitedly and told her mummy that she was going to write a story and draw pictures of their wonderful day out at the park.

Evie told her mummy that she would draw Mr Snowman, Sizzling bacon, the baps, the eggs, the sausages and all the little snowflakes and she would put their names beside them so her mummy would always remember their lovely day in the park.

Evie's mummy looked delighted and said, "Thank you, Evie! That is such a wonderful idea." Then Evie's mummy suggested that together they could stick them into Evie's mummy's memory book, and then they would both have the wonderful memories they had made that day for ever and ever.

Evie was so tired on her return home that she could hardly keep her eyes open.

She wondered when she would see her new friends again and she hoped that Mr Snowman and all the little snowflakes would not melt overnight. Evie climbed into bed and smiled to herself as she remembered the fun they had all had dancing together; she could still see Mr Snowman waving his arms and running all around the park laughing hysterically to himself.

Evie was so glad she had used the magic dust now and Mr Snowman would not be alone. Evie was so tired that night that she fell straight to sleep. When she awoke the next morning, she wondered if she had dreamed it all.

Had Twinkie, Daisy, Bracken, the Sizzling bacon, the Eggs, the Sausages, the Baps and Mr Snowman all been just a dream?

Evie felt her little heart saddening at the thought of never seeing her new friends again or her mummy never getting a chance to dance again. Then Evie suddenly heard her mummy calling up the stairs with an excited voice that it was Christmas day. With a heavy heart, Evie threw on her dressing gown and walked down the stairs; she didn't care that there would be no sizzling bacon or lovely presents.

Evie gasped and gave a squeal of delight and did a little, happy dance. Santa had come even though she had used all of her magic dust and underneath the tree there were lots of brightly wrapped presents. Evie quickly tore the paper off one present after another, after another, throwing the wrapping all over the floor as she did so.

Evie loved her new doll and she loved the felt tip pens and the huge colouring book but she particularly loved the new bike Santa had brought for her. Evie's mummy started to tidy up the wrapping paper.

As she bent down, she noticed another parcel behind the tree; she looked surprised as she did not remember buying or wrapping that present. Evie's mummy looked at the beautifully wrapped sparkly present and shook her head in confusion. Evie's mummy thought she must have bought it and then forgotten. she tutted at herself. The present was labelled to Evie but didn't say who it was from. Evie's mummy felt all around the present and shook it gently before handing it to Evie. Evie's mummy shook her head and thought to herself that there was no one else here so she definitely must have bought it even if she didn't remember doing it.

Evie's mummy watched as Evie ripped the present open and put her hand over her mouth. Evie gasped in delight when out fell Sizzling bacon, Daisy and a huge snowman dressed in an orange shirt and a brown suit with the buttons missing off the blazer: it was Mr Snowman.

Evie was delighted to see her new friends. She hugged all of them together very tightly, Evie now knew that it had all been real.

She hadn't been dreaming after all and best of all she now knew that there was a land that existed without dementia; where Evie's mummy could dance and sing to her heart's content whenever she wanted to. Evie thought excitedly that if it was possible there, then one day it would be possible here too.

Evie smiled to herself thinking that no one would ever get dementia again and her mummy would never get lost or forget where she was going and no one would ever laugh at her mummy ever again

Evie looked at her mummy's smiling face and she knew in her heart that she loved her mummy, dementia or not, monsters on her bed or not, sizzling bacon or not.

Her mummy would always be her mummy and nothing could ever change that. Out of the corner of Evie's eye she thought she saw Daisy smiling at Mr Snowman.

Evie and Evie's mummy stared at Mr Snowman, Daisy and Sizzling bacon in shock. Mr Snowman was so excited that he could not contain his laughter any longer. The shocked expressions on Evie's and her mummy's faces were hilarious.

Mr Snowman suddenly jumped up and did a funny, little dance all around the living room. Mr Snowman then bent down on one knee and looked up into Evie's and Evie's mummy's astonished faces and then in an excited voice, he told Evie's mummy that they had all come to stay with them, and that Twinkie, Bracken and the others were waiting for them at the park to have lots more exciting adventures.

Evie was so thrilled she threw herself into Mr Snowman's arms knocking them both down onto the floor, giggling and laughing. Evie hugged Mr Snowman and thanked him for coming to stay and asked if they could hurry up and go to the park to see her other friends?

Mr Snowman said of course they can, but first they all had to sit around the breakfast table in Evie's mummy's lovely, bright red kitchen and have some delicious, hot, sizzling, crispy bacon.

Mr Snowman was startled when Sizzling bacon suddenly jumped to his feet and tried to get away so quickly that his dangly legs refused to move the way he wanted them to. Sizzling bacon was running and running and running but not going anywhere; he was rooted to the spot and he looked desperate to get away.

Eventually, Sizzling bacon's gangly legs could run no further and he fell flat on his face on the floor with a great, big thump.

Sizzling bacon turned his crispy head and sorrowfully looked up at Mr Snowman, with a very worried, squeaky, sounding voice. Sizzling bacon begged Mr Snowman and the others, "Please, please, please ... do not eat me all up." Mr Snowman looked confused but suddenly he realised what Sizzling bacon had thought and he let out a great, big, belly laugh.

Mr Snowman reached out and gripped Sizzling bacon's, crispy hands and helped Sizzling bacon to his feet. Mr Snowman gently clapped Sizzling bacon on his back and fondly said, "NOT YOU SIZZLE! You are my friend; we would never eat you."

Giggling a little, Evie asked, "How could you ever think that we would eat you all up? There is plenty of bacon in mummy's bright red kitchen, just waiting to be sizzled."

Reviews

ANNE Scott's debut short Sizzling Bacon ... Primarily to explain to children what Dementia is. The genre Anne uses is therefore very child-friendly. Centred around a young girl Evie and her mother who has been diagnosed with dementia. Using unusual characters, understanding of Dementia is told. The loving understanding relationship between mother and daughter. The unusual characters who become friends with the pair once 'what Dementia is', has been explained to them.

Dementia is non-discriminate. Once thought of as an old person's disease. This is not so. This story will inform children indeed but also the adults who read to the children indeed, but also the adults who read to the children. As an adult I had heard of Dementia but until my mother had dementia, I realised how little I understood. Sizzling Bacon–is one of the most heartfelt and kindest short stories I've read. The author's gentle approach to her daughter is overwhelmed by the love and care her daughter shows in return. Evie is a loving daughter with an amazing mother who has dementia but this never separates the love and care they both share in a magical way.

Myrtle George

My heart goes out to both of them as my mother is in early stages of development. This brings me hope that no matter what happens love and support will get us through.

C. McCullough

Sizzling Bacon? Well the title intrigued me so I had to keep reading and although I am not in the target age group! How glad I am that I did. I was diagnosed with early onset dementia in 2012 and I love to hear and read the writings of my friends. I always discover something new, or a reinforcement of something I know.

Anne has used her imagination to write a loving, informative, educational story for children (and adults) using her experience. I loved the relationship between Evie and her mum. Too many children have to deal with dementia and how little support they get. How often do we stop to look at dementia from their perspective?

Not often enough. So, I hope this not only informs children but also adults who may not realise just what children are dealing with when trying to understand dementia.

I loved the use of humour, and together with the magic, it takes away the fears. Anne has separated Evie's Mum from the dementia. She shows Evie's Mum is still the loving mother trying to deal with her worries. The difficulties she has are the disease.

Have a read as it will help parents and grandparents to have important discussions with children about understanding dementia, and shows that the love is still there. And finally, it triggered happy recollections of my childhood Christmas eves, an added bonus for me.

Hilary Doxford

This book has a very personal, thoughtful and sensitive way of helping to explain a parent's diagnosis of dementia in a child-friendly way. I laughed, I cried and felt honoured to be one of the first to read such a beautifully written book.

Angela MacDonald

Barnardo's Young Carers' Service

THE END